This Book Belongs to

. . . .

To Mum, Dad, Will and Joe.
And, of course, little Sammy - A.C.

ORCHARD BOOKS
First published in Great Britain in 2022
by The Watts Publishing Group

Text and illustrations © Alice Courtley 2022

The moral rights of the author have been asserted.

All rights reserved

A CIP catalogue record of this book
is available from the British Library.

HB ISBN: 978 1 40836 419 2
PB ISBN: 978 1 40836 420 8

10 9 8 7 6 5 4 3 2 1

Printed and bound in China.

Orchard Books
An imprint of Hachette Children's Group
Part of The Watts Publishing Group Limited

Carmelite House
50 Victoria Embankment
London EC4Y 0DZ

An Hachette UK Company
www.hachette.co.uk
www.hachettechildrens.co.uk

FSC
www.fsc.org
MIX
Paper from
responsible sources
FSC® C104740

ORCHARD

LOST IN THE CITY

Alice Courtley

Maya loved her family. They made a perfect three — just Maya, Gran and little Sammy. They lived in a cosy house hidden away in a peaceful street. There was nowhere Maya would rather be.

Gran was an adventurer. She was always telling Maya and Sammy epic tales of her life in the city.

She ate exotic foods . . .

danced with beautiful people . . .

and she explored
the world in
big buildings
that housed
the past.

Maya thought that Gran was **very brave.**

One day, Gran said, **"We're going on an adventure.
We're going to the city!"**

But Maya didn't want to go. The city sounded different and big and
very, very scary. She liked it at home with Sammy, where she felt safe
and she knew where everything was. But Gran was so excited . . .

"Can Sammy come too?" Maya asked.

"The city is much too big for a little kitten like Sammy," Gran said. "Don't worry, love, I'll look after you. Oh, look at the time – we're going to be late!"

They ran out so fast that Maya didn't even have time to pet Sammy goodbye.

As the city loomed closer, Maya started to feel smaller and smaller.

"Next stop, darling. Don't forget your bag," said Gran.

Maya bent down to get her bag when . . .

CITY →

Sammy, how did you get here?

The city is much too big for such a small kitten, Maya thought.

"Don't worry, Sammy, I'll look after you," she pulled her
bag close and took Gran's hand.

"We need to keep our energy up for today," Gran said, leading them to a café. With cake in her tummy and Sammy nearby, Maya started to feel less scared.

It was almost fun watching the people outside.
The girls in their bright clothes, the boy with his
guitar, the funny man and his funny little dog,
who was barking at . . .

. . . a small orange kitten!

Maya had to look after Sammy.

"Let's go, Gran!" she shouted, and off they went.

"That cake has worked wonders for you," Gran smiled. Maya could just spy Sammy in the market when Gran stopped. "What gorgeous flowers," she said, "and these mangoes smell divine."

But there was no time for mangoes.

"Gran, quick!" Maya insisted.

"We need to go to—"

"—the library!" The library looked like a wonderful place to get lost in, and Sammy was definitely lost.

"Oh, let's check some of these out," Gran said, picking out a few books.

Then Maya spotted a flash of orange.

"Come on, Gran. Let's go to—"

"—the department store."

"That wasn't on our plan," said Gran.
"But look at these shoes . . .
and this hat. Let's get matching ones."

"Quick, Gran, outside!"
Maya urged.

"This takes me back," Gran shouted, dancing and making friends. Everyone was smiling, and Maya was starting to smile too when out the corner of her eye she saw a big lion and a small . . .

Sammy!

"Let's go, Gran!"

"Oh, you've found my favourite place in the city," Gran smiled.

"Wait for me."

They ran through the grand hall . . .

into the painting room . . .

and finally, into the sculpture room.

"Oh my, that one has unusual hair,"
wheezed Gran.

It was Sammy — at last! Then . . .

Sammy was nowhere in sight.

"I think it's nearly time for our train now, darling,"
said Gran. Maya couldn't believe she'd lost Sammy.

"We can't go yet, Gran. I need to find—"

"Shh, don't worry, Maya. We'll come back soon. We *all* will."

And then Maya noticed . . .

"Oh, Sammy!"

Maya waited for Gran to get angry, but she didn't.

"You did such a good job looking after him, Maya," said Gran. "But perhaps next time, we should bring a lead."

On the train, they snacked on the food from the market.
It was different from anything Maya had eaten before,
but different tasted surprisingly delicious.

They watched the tall towers twinkle as they rushed
by on their way home. The city was still very big,
but Maya didn't feel so small anymore.

And anyway, she was too busy dreaming
of their next adventure to notice.